This book is dedicated to my Mom and Dad

who never gave up on me.

Letters to Zoë

Dear Zoë,

If you heard that I left, you may be wondering why or perhaps I'm just flattering myself in believing that you would care, or that you even noticed I was gone.

– Wait. I don't want to begin this letter like that. I want to tear this page from my notebook and toss it into the dimming distance as I walk away from the shame of another mistake, but I only have one notebook and every page is precious. I can't throw away what I have already done, but hopefully with what remains I may say what I really feel, instead of impulsively blurting rash nonsense. So, if you are still reading this, perhaps you will be kind enough to let me start again.

Well, I did leave. I am not sure why. The first notion is that I'm running from something. If I am, I could only be running from myself. Then I thought, perhaps I'm trying to run to something or somewhere, but I haven't the faintest idea what or where that could be. Really, I've thought that I just want to run and feel myself flowing into the open.

My life had become overwhelming. I felt like a

jumbled yarn, a string that was knotted in the most inextricable ways. I was pulling at the tangles, but instead of loosening the knots, they would only tighten. I felt strangled in my own constriction. Now I've been living outside for a couple of weeks, standing beneath the open sky, watching the sun passing overhead, and the most soothing sight I have ever seen is the long stretches of highway extending out before me.

The highway is seldom straight, but it's not tangled. It stretches in every direction farther than I can see, disappearing around curves and turns, dissolving into thickening forests, climbing ridges and vanishing into the sky at the horizon and this feels comforting. It gives me hope that there is something beyond the confusion of myself.

The night I left town, I walked to Irondale through the train yard. I have no doubt why they call it Irondale in my mind now. The railroad tracks are splayed out everywhere converging and diverging in an intricacy of switches. The weight of the steel felt to deepen the valley, compact the ground with the burden of freight and squeeze up the surrounding hills that the diesels plowed to the side. Then stretching out on their own, narrowed down to a pair nailed to the timbers of the cross ties, a little rusty on the side but polished smooth where the loads of trains rolled, a few lines veer off and extend into the distance.

I spotted a coal train passing through the yard. Watching the train leave, I kept waiting for a good car to hop aboard. I expected a boxcar with a welcoming open door to appear from around the bend, like in the movies, but that never happened. I realized that if I was looking for a passenger car, I'd need to find another station. Those cars weren't carrying windows and cushions. They were carrying weight. So eventually I decided I had to jump on where I could because the train was building speed and soon it would be going too fast for me to catch a ride.

I lumbered along the track with my bumbling duffle bag bouncing on my shoulder. It was stuffed with a bunch of junk I thought I would need, the cluttering jumble of my life I cling to. The bag's strap bunched the fabric of my shirt and pinched my skin. The cumbrous bulk tugged and pulled me back. Every step I took slipped on the collapsing gravel. The whole endeavor felt ludicrous and absurd. I figured I would slip and the train's steel wheels would cut me in half without the slightest hint of a bump of my body beneath them. Those wheels roll with the senseless, merciless nature of machinery and the only kindness one might find is in the engineer's cautious mind. Then I caught hold of the ladder and the train had me. It carried me. It lifted me off my feet. I felt elation. I felt like I was flying. I felt free.

The train was immense. A long line of bolted and riveted steel and tons and tons of coal. It was like a long spine stripped bone bare. I felt like I was shedding layers of my skin. In the grit of coal, I felt like I was being abrasively cleansed. When the train slowed, the slack in the knuckle couplers would snap tight as one butted against the other. The sound would begin from the back of the train and then ripple up to me and beneath my feet while I sat on the brake platform. I would see the knuckles beneath me, the tiny gap of space between them suddenly close so that there was nothing but steel pressed against steel. And then the snapping would continue all the way to the locomotives. It was like the slow cracking of a long spine. It felt like the release of tension, the tightening and compressing and then a moment of relief. So much that had gathered in me felt to be fluttering off in the past.

The whole time I was riding, it always seemed like we were going straight. I knew the train was twisting around bends because I watched the moon move through the sky, but from where I sat, I couldn't detect any turns. I was a little hesitant about sticking my head out over the edge because I was afraid I might suddenly lose it. I could only see a tiny sliver of trees passing in a blur of velocity as the train creaked and clacked through the country.

I can still hear my dad's voice. He woke as I was leaving. While I walked across the yard, the evening dew sparkling in the moonlight, my feet shuffling tracks through the crystal drops on the carpet of the lawn, I heard him shout, "Weldon! Weldon! Where are you going?" I didn't know what to say. He could certainly see that I had his old army duffle bag and that I was determined to go. I didn't slow down; I didn't look back; I don't know if he heard me, I just called out "Away."

The train stopped at a power plant. Some guy from the railroad walked along the tracks. The beam of his flash light waved with his steps through the settling dust of coal. I slipped off the other side and hid in the shadows. Behind me, I could see the power plant. It looked like a fortress with towering chimneys rising through the fog of lights, hissing and whistling while it boiled inside. I suppose it was a good thing the guy made sure the train was clear. If I had been riding when the cars dumped their loads, the thick dust of the coal would have smothered my lungs and my spark would have been snuffed.

I don't mean to bore you with these details. The reason I'm writing you is not to give you a description of what I'm doing. I wanted to write you because I was concerned that you may have thought that I was leaving because of you. Again, I hope this isn't a vain assumption. We have known each other for years and have been close friends. It is funny though, you were always with Ray and I've liked you for so long, but I never wanted to interfere with what you two had. I never wanted to impose upon the relationship you two shared.

Now that's changed. That last night we went out I had a wonderful time. Ray's gone and I suppose we could have gotten to know one another in a way different than ever before. Believe me, I wanted that more than anything. Pardon me if I am being assumptive again, but I had a feeling that you may have felt that way too. I didn't mean to brush you off for the past several years. Or rather, I guess I did, but it wasn't because I didn't like you, I just don't like interfering with other people's relationships. I feel like I want to tighten the bonds between people, to help bring people together, to help us understand one another, and I couldn't see myself ever accomplishing this if I was willing to break a bond between two people I knew well and cared for.

That night we went out was wonderful. I was surprised that you were willing to climb the fire tower with me. It has the most amazing view of the city, but all I wanted to look at was you. Everything else was just a backdrop for your beauty. I have probably climbed that tower a hundred times, but climbing it with you was like nothing before. I felt like we were looking down over the airplanes soaring

7

through the sky. When we held hands, I felt like wings were unfolding beneath us. It was wonderful.

Now though, my scene is far from romantic. I'm camped in a huge drainage ditch in Southern California. There were flash floods recently and apparently they were very severe. There is debris everywhere. The person who drove me here warned me about the floods. He said that I wouldn't even know they're coming most times because the rain falls in the mountains. All you can see is the flashing of lighting in the distance. But then you'll hear the thunder of the water rushing down, tumbling the trunks of trees and rolling boulders.

Nearby, there is an amusement park. I can see the tops of the roller coasters. Sometimes I hear the gleeful screams of exhilaration as the cars gather speed with the drop of the ride, then again slow to crest another peak and then repeat and repeat, a pulse dwindling to the end. Then my eyes drop from the banners waving in the distance, and my ears close from the merriment wafting in the wind and all I see around me is the chaos from the floods, piles of trees torn from the hills and smashed against the bases of bridges, the carnage of deluge, the detritus of debacle. I do like being close to the park though, even if I'm on the other side of the fence. I find comfort in witnessing other people enjoy life. They remind me that it is possible.

Your friend,

Weldon

Dear Zoë,

You are on my mind all the time. Please don't take that the wrong way though. I'm not obsessing. I just can't help it. Every time I see something beautiful I think of you. Every time I feel alone I think of you. Memories of you are soothing. They give my life some sense of steadiness. Your image is firmly fixed in my mind while on the highway everything is always passing by. I am happy though, perhaps happier than I have ever been. There is an exhilarating sensation in liberation.

The other day, I made a point to take off my shoes and socks and walk on the bare ground on my bare feet. I can't remember the last time I did this. Typically the cool earth was beyond my touch. It was covered with layers of concrete and asphalt while I was enclosed in buildings behind slamming and locking doors. I would cover myself in layers of clothes, bunched behind buttons, clinched in zippers and strapped with belts. I would cover myself for comfort, for decency, for fashion while I scuffled and squeaked in molded rubber soles. I want to touch the world and feel the world as it is, perhaps then I may begin to feel more a part of it.

Still, standing along the sides of the roads there is a sense of detachment and displacement. The roadside resembles so much of life that I knew. I'm standing still, watching the heat vapors welt from the asphalt while one person after another whizzes by in their encapsulated lives. There is so much mystery in each one of us. I always find each encounter intriguing and alluring but the intersections of our lives are often brief and the barriers and enclosures that encase us often seem impenetrable.

Right now, my only means to inspire any intrigue and allure for anyone to stop and open their vehicle to me is the sight of desperation. My only means are others' pity. I have reduced my capacity to others sympathy for a lonely figure stranded along the parched highway. With my thumb up in the air, I'll often look down on myself to see dingy clothes dangling from some mysterious figure underneath. I feel like a different person.

I was considering how we typically introduce ourselves to one another. I have heard people will often form an opinion of a person within the first seconds of meeting. This seems absurd though. I know from my own experiences, the time that I am the least like myself is in the awkward encounters of introductions. That stranger doesn't meet me as I am, but rather how I present myself. Instead of seeing me in an open and comfortable disposition, I am seen as withdrawn and wary. That person is not meeting me; that person is meeting a deflection of me.

This made me consider a peculiar way I behave in some situations. I have always thought it odd that when I meet two different people, if I am especially interested in one of those persons, I will often direct my attention toward the person I am less interested. Perhaps I do this so I can indirectly exhibit myself, so I can portray myself in a way I feel most relaxed and natural. But then my demeanor becomes more of an avoidance of awkwardness than an expression of my interest. It is like pursuing my interest by dismissing it, as if everything I seek in life can only be reached obliquely and directness only chases any hope of engagement away.

Saying this, I wonder if I am only making some

complicated explanation of the real issue that is on my mind. As I have said, I think of you often and feel deeply for you. But saying this and more importantly, knowing this and being this, my thoughts dissipate into the vast distance I've placed between us. Why would I travel across the continent before I feel I can speak to you directly? Why would I think I had to run away to approach you? Why can I only say what I really feel when we are far beyond each other's touch?

I remember when you would tell me about the books you were reading. As you described them, I could see worlds of wonder fantastically unfolding. I know I've told you that I have since read many of the books that you described, but I don't know if I ever told you that much of what I was seeking through those books was not really the books themselves or what they contained in their type, I was searching for what intrigued you, what drew you into those pages as if I could follow the long line of each story and trace an impression of your life. It was like every time I turned a page, the tips of my fingers were gently touching another edge of your life as I fluttered deeper inside.

14

Zoë

It is funny looking up over what I have written. I can see how the style of my handwriting changes through certain parts of the letter. The beginning looks stilted and rigidly self-aware, each word laboriously carved from the emptiness of uncertainty. Then as I trace my thoughts of you, following your crisp and clear outline in my mind, strolling along the paths of memories of what is transpiring in my life, envisioning you with me while I search inside myself in hopes of finding something that is true, something that is worthy of presenting to you, the tip of my pen whirls like the wind and the script flows relaxed and intact.

I suppose I will seal this note in an envelope now. I bought some stamps in the last town. In the next one, I will mail this to you. I hope all is well. I am doing fine.

Your Friend,

Weldon

Dear Zoë,

The lapse of time in these letters feels odd. Earlier today, I mailed the last letter I wrote you, but that last letter is what I felt a week ago. Now that I have sent it, I am feeling completely different from different experiences. Having mailed the last letter today, I don't know when I will be able to mail this one I'm writing now. I will pass through another town somewhere down the road where I can drop it in a post office box, but by then, this overwhelming immediacy of the present will have past, as it is detached within the envelope in which it will be sealed. I feel that all I can offer you is what I have been and I want to show you what I am.

Spending the last month hitchhiking, I am still a little intrigued as to what motivates some people into giving me a ride. I would never expect others to detach themselves from their interest, pause in the course of their lives, lift their eyes from the fixation of their destinations and pull to the side of the road and offer me a seat in their world, a role as a momentary companion in their journey. I certainly don't look respectable. My clothes are dusty and grungy. I haven't shaved in a while and I am not sure what my hair looks like. In fact, I have been consciously avoiding looking at my own reflection. It seems the more I linger upon myself, the more I displace myself from what surrounds me.

Every time I get into a car, there are always the same obvious questions. The first question almost everybody asks is where I'm going. It's a simple question. We're both on the road travelling, so it's safe to say we're both trying to get somewhere. It's the way we interact, we search for relatable topics to initiate and hopefully to sustain some type of communication. But this question about where I'm going, baffles me. I want to say "know-where", but that's just confusing. Really, I haven't even tried to imagine a destination. I hardly even think of a direction. I simply see the roads extending in every different way and although I know I'm only seeing tiny portions of the world, perhaps someday I may be able to piece those portions together into something whole.

Through my travels, I have realized how nebulous a

silent person can be. When I sit in someone's car and remain quiet, they often grow wary of me. It is odd because I always thought of silence as crystal clear. I tell people that I prefer to remain silent because when I talk I can only hear myself. I am the last person I want to listen to. I'm already stuck with me for life, at least let me listen to someone else.

But speaking is how we share our thoughts, how we open our inner worlds for others. It gives people a sense of our being, of our interests and intentions. If a person is kind enough to give me a ride, at least I can set them at ease and not simply sit like a lurking, malingering mystery in the corner of their eye while they drive. I developed a routine in telling stories of recent experiences and through this I divulge the thoughts that occupy my mind and guide my life.

I suppose this is somewhat similar to what I'm doing through these letters. I know I am easily distracted and I must sound incredibly self-centered since all I am doing is writing about myself, but I must admit, the more I think about it, the more I realize how little I know about you. I don't want to jump to conclusion and try to tell you about yourself, or talk presumptuously about us. Rather I only hope that I might show you something of myself, something that may gain your trust so that you may feel comfortable with me.

The other day I was thinking about talking with you. I was imagining you asking me what qualities that I enjoyed about you and my response was that I only hoped that you would have the patience to listen to me for a lifetime because the qualities of your life extend far beyond where I can see and I would never hope to find an end to them. But the qualities that I cherish the most are the ones that I could never describe. They would only be diminished if I tried to put them in words with my feeble attempts at description. They are the qualities that are yours and yours alone and that I can only remain silent and witness because the only way I feel they could ever be accurately described is how they are perfectly exhibited through your life.

Then thinking this, I can't help but watch my pen scratch across this page to see how coarsely I express myself. It is like I am trying to squeeze what I feel through this pen, to wring my life through this tiny tip and extend it across the numb silence of distance. I see the pen dance in my hand, but all that remains are these ink stains across the otherwise blank page. As I transpose what I feel on the page, the breadth of reality, the fullness of existence, the living energy, the warmth of breath, the pulsing of blood, the pounding of my heart, the buzzing in my head, I watch the words turn oddly indecipherable and stretch thin into tiny squiggles that could never contain all I want to give.

I am rambling now, forgive me. But I was trying to express some of the mystery I am feeling and the wonder I am experiencing as I encounter so many people and try to understand them and present myself in a way that I may be understood. This is where an experience I had earlier today strikes me like a hammer on a bell, a sharp blow that quivers with resonant sound rippling through my body.

In the past town I had an encounter with a person and the encounter was not the best, to say the least. In fact, at the time it was a little scary, but now it feels different, in some way the disturbance has settled into a clarity that is hushed and gravely somber.

Before I describe it, I must reassure you that I am

perfectly safe and I am taking every precaution possible.

As I was walking out of the town after dropping the last letter in the mail box, a car pulled up beside me and the driver began taunting me. I tried to ignore him. I wasn't going to react in a hostile way because that was the reaction he was trying to provoke. Through these travels I am constantly reminded of the brief lengths and the narrow breadths in which our lives are confined. Even as free as I feel now, I am still following the road; I am still riding in cars that are opened to me through other's generosity. But here I was in a situation where I could definitely choose how I would act, how I would behave and which direction I would go and I was not going to allow this person to make this decision for me.

Eventually, he pulled the car in front of me to obstruct my path. I began walking around the car and he jumped out and continued taunting me, even pushing me a few times and tugging at my bag. At first, I resorted to some sense of self-pity. I kept thinking, "Why is this happening to me? What did I do to this guy? What did I do to deserve this?" Yet, I decided to remain silent and kept trying to walk by, but he persisted. Finally I realized I had to react in some way. First, I stopped. This prompted him to pause while he tried anticipating my next move, bracing himself for the worst. Then I said, "Hey, how about this, you do you and I'll do me, OK. I'm just passing through." After all, I was simply covering ground, not trying to claim it.

He froze in his tracks for a moment, perhaps he drooped his head a bit, but I didn't pay any attention. He had been immobilized for a second, perhaps to consider what I had said, and this gave me the opportunity to take a few steps around him and continue on my way. When he drove off, he yelled a disgruntled something or nothing out the window, but the sound of his voice had dispersed before his car disappeared around the corner.

As I walked away, my mind rushed and reeled with thoughts of the incident. I kept rolling the situation around in my head, roiling it in the streams of my thought hoping to uncover some explanations or reach some clarity. As I did this though, I kept swirling down a murky maelstrom in my mind.

Then a thought occurred to me. All of the sudden I

realized how fortunate I am. Of course I was fortunate that the situation didn't escalate into violence, but beyond this, I felt how fortunate I am in myself as myself, despite my troubles. No doubt, this guy had shown me a very ugly part of himself. What he projected upon me, even in the brevity of that encounter, is a part of himself that he lives with every day.

I had it easy. I could walk away. I could allow that anger and pain to dissipate into my past. But he clings to it and it clings to him. The guy definitely had some major problems and I was not going to allow myself to become part of those problems. Those problems were his. I was not going to make them mine too. After all, there are already far too many tormented lives in the world.

Your Friend,

Weldon

March 25

Dear Zoë,

You may be wondering where I am. Much of the time, I can honestly say I don't know. I suppose I could check a map, but I'm not on a map.

I don't think I mentioned where I was when I wrote the last letter. Most of the time I don't know the names of the towns, but while I'm there I don't need to call them by their name. I don't need a label to jog them from my memory. You may have noticed the postage stamps. If so, you would at least know where I mailed the letters. I see the town; I see the people; I can trace the encompassing horizon with my eyes, but in a way, you have a better idea of where I've been than I do. Perhaps it is like I see the place and you see the location.

Right now I do know I'm in Lone Pine, California. It is a small town settled in the Inyo Valley just east of Mount Whitney which is the tallest mountain in the contiguous states. I am looking at it now, pausing while I write this, staring up at its immensity looming above me.

As I approached the mountain on my last ride and

watched it arise in the distance, I felt an overwhelming draw. I suppose it is the adventurer in me. I felt compelled to climb it, to reach the wind whittled rock at the top and pull myself up to stand on my tiptoes at its peak and reach into the heights of the sky.

My ride dropped me off outside of town and I watched the car veer off and drive away from the fork in the road. I began to walk, but there seemed to be no direct way to reach the mountain. The road is clear and open, but all along the sides there are fences and obstacles. The mountain irresistibly beckoned me but all I encountered was barbed wire and private property. At one point I decided to jump a fence and began cutting a direct path through a corral. In no time though, I found myself ankle deep in manure. It was a nightmare.

Returning to the road, I decided to walk into town and see if I could find a side road that would take me to the base or some trailhead. In this, my atlas was useless. It doesn't list any of the small roads, only the major highways and the interstates.

I found myself walking in circles. Directly in front of

me was the most colossal object, a mountain that can be seen for miles, a feature of the terrain that can be seen from space. It was all I could see, but there seemed to be no way to reach it.

It reminded me of how I've known you for so many years. All the time I knew you, you were so immediate, so close, but you were always with Ray. Sometimes you were all I could think about, but there seemed to be no way I could reach you without violating some type of trust that I wanted to respect, a trust that I held for both of you and what you two had together. Oddly though, now that I am on the other side of the continent, I feel I can reach you and speak to you like I never have before. This reminds me of the other night when I was staring at the moon. I kept wondering if you might be looking up at the moon too. Then even as far away as we are from one another, that instant, that glimmering moment gazing along those silvery strands streaming through the cool night sky, that may have been a moment when we were together.

I wasn't able to reach the mountain. However, while I climbed some surrounding hills, I had an astonishing insight. While I walked, I stumbled upon a new frontier of my own potential. The sun was glaring in my eyes as I struggled from underneath my heavy and bulging bag while I schlepped up the hills. Carrying all that I own, all that I have to sustain me, to shelter and comfort me, I staggered into the shadow of the mountain and the glare was gone and I could see. The soft breeze chilled over my skin in a sign of relief. I thought, "Look Weldon, you can move mountains. You can move mountains in front of the sun by stepping into their shade."

Call this an angle of view or perspective, but it provided a magnificent revelation. Our scope is narrow. Much is to be said of what we can align within our sight.

Then atop one of the hills, I watched the evening stretching to the east as the surface of the earth spun into its shadow. With the change in temperature, the wind began rushing over the hills. Then I noticed three crows gliding through the air above me, floating on their wings and the wind. They looked like they were having fun surfing a wave through the sky's untouchable blue. People tend to think of crows as ominous, but they always seem jocular to me. They're sociable. I hardly ever see anyone of them alone and they're always talking together. They seem like they always have friends and I like that about them. It makes me feel like we're not always alone.

When I was a kid, I used to try finding their nests. They are conspicuous in the open, even to the point of being obnoxious, but they are very secretive about their homes. In the spring time I would watch them gathering materials to weave their nests for their clutches of eggs. But they are clever birds. They would always know when I was following.

I doubt I would have been able to climb the trees to reach them anyway. They travel paths that my steps are too heavy to tread. They walk on their hands; their palms are lofting fans of feathers. Sometimes they touch me with their shadows, lids that blink over the sun the instant they pass over me. Perhaps that is the only way they may reach me. Perhaps that is the only way I may reach you, outstretched with the shadows of my thoughts written as scripted silhouettes and cast upon the page. Or perhaps the spaces between the letters say more, perhaps the spaces are the open sky and the sunlight that shines through the unsettled flight of my life.

This time, I have done something different than with the previous letters. As I have been writing this, I am actually sitting on the sidewalk in Lone Pine leaning up against the mail drop box. I want you to receive this note as close to this moment as possible. I want this letter to zip to you without any delay and perhaps in this, I may approach you, like how you can talk on the phone and even though the conversation is traveling over thousands of miles of wire, bouncing between satellites in space, you can still close your eyes and imagine that the person is whispering directly into your ear, almost as if you can feel the warmth of their breath which is so much more real than words.

Your Friend,

Weldon

Dear Zoë,

One of the wonders of traveling is watching the terrain and even the climate change while I move. Sometimes in the cars, I convince myself I am sitting still, fixed within an enclosed space and the world is simply transforming around me. Moving from arid regions to places with more moisture is like watching spring arrive as the dry, scrubby land rises with pines over the course of a single day.

Other times I am intrigued by the motion. Standing along the roadside, waiting for a ride, the world feels settled and still while the cars dash past. Inside the cars, the stillness is compacted into a compartment while the world slowly drifts by outside. I cannot say which I prefer, except that I am grateful to have realized the difference.

I left California the other day and now I'm in Reno, Nevada. I only left home with $150 and that is almost gone so I figured I would head into one of the cities and try finding a temporary job to replenish my funds. I was lucky enough to find a room in one of the missions along Main Street. When I walk out the front door, I make a left turn and within a few blocks I walk beneath a glittering and sparkling arch that says, "Biggest Little City in the World". And then further on, the strip leads me along the flashing lights of the casinos all vying to bedazzle and allure every passing eye. The guy who gave me a ride here said it is fairly easy to get a job in the city, so I have been walking through the streets all day submitting applications. The guy also gave me a pointer about gambling. He said: "The worse thing a person can do is win."

The Mission is an old Victorian house. I have been staying out of the cities while I've been gone because I feel safer sleeping in obscure places along the roads. There are too many people in the cities and it doesn't feel safe sleeping in the streets. I was fortunate to find this place which is somewhat safe and allows me to secure my stuff while I stroll out in my jaunts around town prospecting for work.

They have several books here and I spend the evenings reading, continuing my adventures as I explore what the pages contain. I found one that is very interesting, but it is missing the first several pages. Apparently something very important happened in the opening of the book because it is constantly referred to, but I am trying to figure out what it was as I read deeper into the novel.

In some ways, I was wondering how this resembles my own life. Like most everyone, I cannot remember any of my first few years. Sometimes I want to think that my outlook on life was more pristine then, that my mind had yet to be muddled with the confusions and reduced to the routines of day to day existence. Then the entirety of my life is simply an attempt to return to that pristine state that is too perfect to remember, that encompasses more than our conscious capacity can contain. I once heard that when we grow older, our sleeping habits return to the rhythms we experienced when we were infants, that our lives slowly wind back to their beginnings where they end. Perhaps then we may awake, completely and entirely, but then again, by that time, we may be so tired, we may only want to sleep.

This puzzles me though. I remember when I was about six I told my mother that I never wanted to have any children because I felt that life is so painful that I could never allow myself to subject another person to it. I still wonder if that is the best choice. We are animals; reproduction is an essential aspect of our existence. I keep remembering one of the lines from the fragments of Epicurus' writings. I cannot remember it exactly, but it addresses the reality of our individual existence and states how we are simply drops of water in a big river. This feels odd now, because I am in a scorched terrain and a gritty city. I tend to tell myself that I am simply a segment in a series and in this case, how could I be so arrogant to declare myself the conclusion?

A more exciting note though, I was in my first earth quake the other day. It was mild, only about 3.1 on the Richter scale, but it was still quite a shake. Everybody talks about the earthquakes in California, but I never thought I'd experience one in Nevada. It made me think of the basis of my life and the portions of the world, society and myself, that I rely upon for a sense of stability. There couldn't be anything that I would believe to be more stable and secure than the ground itself, and then all of the sudden I began to feel it move beneath me.

The desert is nice though. The air is crisp and you can see for miles in every direction, at least when I can peer out of the maze of Reno's towering walls. Sometimes down the long lines of the avenues, I can see the hills rising beyond the reach of the city. They remind me that outside is always as close as the nearest door.

Your Friend,

Weldon

Dear Zoë,

Talking with you the other day was the greatest pleasure I've ever felt. In fact, I feel like I am still glowing from our conversation. The sound of your voice is the most beautiful music. I felt like my life had grown very cold and it has warmed with the fondness of your thoughts. I am also glad that you are enjoying my letters. I was a little concerned. I didn't know if they were boring you or if you might have begun to think that I was being obsessive in some way. Writing these letters have been an immense help for me, providing me the opportunity to share my thoughts with someone I feel I can trust and who will not jump to rash conclusions if I say something that might come across in a confused manner. If this ever is the case, you can rest assured that the confusion is entirely my own because I know that even the vaguest notions that I could ever try to express to you would be understood with the clarity which I remember seeing in your eyes.

I am still in Reno but I am planning on leaving soon. They cleaned out the Mission's storage the other day.

Apparently people are always leaving things here when they depart and never returning to claim them. Occasionally they clear out the space in the storage, I suppose to accommodate more things for people to abandon. In the pile I was able to find a backpack which will be a huge help for me. It will certainly make my load much easier to bear.

I mailed the army duffle bag back to my dad and thanked him for letting me use it. I'm sure his least concern would have been retaining an old army duffle bag when he watched his son walk out of the house in the middle of the night and disappear into the darkness. But I couldn't just leave it here to be hauled away in the next load to the dump.

While going through my things, I noticed how much excess I was still hauling around. For so many years, I have thought of all of the things that I want and this has begun to concern me. If I am only thinking about what I want and what I do not have, how could I know what I am?

For the time being I know I love traveling; I love meeting so many different people and spanning such a broad range of locations. Every time I walk to work, I cross the railroad tracks that pass through town. Sometimes I pause on the tracks and look down the length of the rails heading west toward the distant mountains. I wonder if there is somewhere those lines meet, as if those parallel rails bend together somewhere to touch, just like they seem to do in the distance at the tip of my vision. But this makes me worry too because I wonder if there is a place where those lines meet, those lines that seem to run side by side forever while I've walked along them, if they could bend toward one another to touch, they could just as easily veer away from one another forever.

Often I must wait for trains to pass because it is a busy freight line. Someone told me that I can hop on those trains and they will take me over the Sierra Nevada range all the way to Sacramento. I must admit, that every time I see the train I think of doing just that. What is more, I know it; I've done it. For me, it is more than a thought. I have made it a reality. Not only do I think about doing, I know that I can. I can do anything I want, but what do I need, and what is needed of me?

As for myself it seems I have found an excellent way to determine my own necessities because if I really do need something, then I must be willing to carry it and to strap it to my back and to lug it through my life. These travels are an excellent opportunity to pare down my life and see if I may be able to determine what is essential for me and perhaps then, what is essential of me. I truly feel I am winnowing through the chaff of my existence in search of the grain of my life's essence.

Working in the casino has been interesting. As I mentioned when we talked on the phone, I am working as a porter on the graveyard shift. The layout of the floors is designed to be confusing. All the walls are mirrors that scramble a person's orientation and magnify the excitement because whenever anything happens, whenever people lift their arms up in celebration or whenever lights start flashing "jackpot", it is not just one event but a myriad of reflections of that event.

People do look like they're having a lot of fun, which is good. But sometimes it is saddening because I will arrive at my shift at midnight and see people sitting at the machines and then when I leave in the morning at eight, they're still sitting at the same machines, pushing the same buttons, pulling the same levers, feeding money into the mechanical devices that ring and ding and flash in response.

As I weave through the players, I'm pulling my handle for money too, but the handle I'm pulling is attached to a broom. There may be no sweepstakes, but there is definitely plenty of sweeping and although the coin wrappers I gather are empty, I get a steady check at the end of every week.

Every day when I return to the mission to sleep, I can still hear the bells in my head. By the time I awake, they are generally gone. I guess I need those lapses of rest to settle the raucous shifts in my thoughts.

I should end this now. I found another interesting book here and I want to finish it before I leave in a couple of days. I hope all is well, and like I said, I really enjoyed talking with you the other day. Take care of yourself.

Your Friend,

Weldon

Dear Zoë,

As I had, if not how I had, intended, I left Reno. I decided that jumping a train didn't sound like a good idea this time. Although I would have been able to traverse the Sierra Nevada range easily, people told me Sacramento, especially around the train yards, can be very dangerous. I have done what I needed to do in Reno. So I walked down the highway until I was whisked away with a ride.

I am grateful for the opportunity to earn some cash and return to my travels, but the job became disgusting in a literal sense. I was transferred to the loading dock where I had to open every bag of trash and search for any items that may have been maliciously thrown away and would cost the casino money. Primarily, I was retrieving plates people would throw in the garbage after eating at the buffet.

I suppose people do this in resentment. Perhaps people lost money and they want to try burning the casino in return. Of course none of the casinos would have anybody's money if people didn't voluntarily give it to them. In reality though, they don't really do anything to hurt the casinos.

They just make some guy like me have to rummage through the garbage and dig out the plates from the muck and slop of discarded food for minimum wage.

It reminds me of a time when I was a child, some kids grabbed my baseball cap and buried it in a bag of lime that was used to mark the boundaries on the little league baseball field. I dug it out and ran out of the shed blindly swinging my fists, but the only person I hit was someone who had nothing to do with it. There is no doubt we all suffer injustice at times, but when we rashly lash out against it, we just hurt ourselves worse as we displace our frustrations on someone else.

I could be wrong about the plates though. There are probably other reasons they are intentionally or accidentally thrown away. Surely it's not all driven by resentment, because I would often find money in the garbage too.

Right now I'm in Northern California somewhere around an old timber town called Weed. I am not sure how far away the town is; I am not sure how much farther in any direction anything is, that is except for the wide open beauty that immediately surrounds me and seems to extend endlessly.

Someone dropped me off last night along highway 97 and I began walking away from the road to sleep for the night. While I walked I found an old section of the highway that had been abandoned some time ago for an alternate and probably more direct route. I sat for hours on the road beneath the bright full moon.

When I was small I had a huge project, or at least to me it was an extraordinarily expansive engineering enterprise. I constructed an elaborate road system in my parents' back yard. I'd spend hours scooting my wheeled toys around those roads and routes I'd made. One time, my parents had some work done on the house and the contractors left half of a bag of cement mix after they finished the job. I couldn't have been more excited. I got my little plastic bucket and began mixing up a batch. Then I began paving the streets I had ploughed through the dirt behind the house. I thought I had really developed something grand at the time. I even found some white paint to brush on the stripes that separated the lanes.

Then the next night, there was a thunderstorm. When I

went outside the next day, I found that the rain had washed away most of the roads I had laid. I was bewildered. I couldn't understand it. From all the roads I had seen in my life as a child, they all gave me the impression of being permanent, as if they would never move, as if they would be there forever.

Then more, sometime later my parents had sod laid in the back yard. I can remember how excited my mom was when we got a lawn but I was shattered. I couldn't understand it. They had completely covered my entire road system. There was something that I had spent so much time developing and improving and elaborating and to me it was the biggest thing in the world. Then all of the sudden I find out that it had been completely erased and that no one else had even realized it was there.

Then while I sat reminiscing about these matters, I kept looking down the old, abandoned road in the moonlight. I was sitting right beside a huge pothole and through the pothole I could see the different layers of the highway. The asphalt was stratified like sediment. Then I saw how the desert brush was beginning to grow over the sides and how the road was slowly crumbling away without being maintained. All of the sudden, it was no longer a road to me. I realized that while I walk along the highways, I would notice so many of the features that are manmade - the roads, the signs, the buildings, the gutters and the grates. And then I would notice everything else. I would make this specific distinction between the road and the landscape. Then while I sat upon this road I noticed how it was nothing more than another geological feature. It had been produced just like anything else and it didn't seem to matter if it had been laid out by the hands of humanity or whether it was a distorted convolution of the crust of the planet; it is all shaped by nature, and just as the plants grow thorns for other creatures, so do they grow flowers and fruit.

Your Friend,

Weldon

May 8

Dear Zoë,

You may need to bear with me because this letter may be fairly long. Now that I consider this, it's a strange statement. I certainly have a lot to say. I had some exciting experiences the last couple of weeks and I want to tell you everything, but as I am writing now, the pages are blank. Yet, when you find this letter in the mail, you will feel the thick bundle of pages the envelope contains. When you flip through the pages, you will see the looping and dashing lines of ink scrawled over them. Then as you read this and only as you read this, now it may be complete.

I left Northern California a couple of weeks ago. I camped out for a day or two outside of Klamath Falls and then began heading into the Cascade Range. I caught a ride up to the mountain pass with an interesting guy.

While we were riding, he kept telling me that I was doing a great thing. That when I am older and I look back at these travels I will always cherish them. Then he began to tell me that he had always wished he had done something adventurous in his youth, hitchhiking around the country or

49

around Europe, joining the Peace Corps or whatever. I was astonished. It was saddening to hear him say this as if he felt that he would never have a chance to live his dreams, that he had no hopes of fulfillment, that he considered his life practically over.

I began to tell him about my aunt. I am not sure if you ever met my dad's sister, she lives out of state, but she had apparently always wanted to become a doctor. But she married while she was young and dropped out of college to live a domestic life. About fifteen years ago, her husband died of Leukemia. After she mourned the loss, she decided to pursue her dream and become a doctor. She returned to college. She must have been in her late thirties and eventually made it into medical school. Now, she is in fact a practicing medical doctor.

I remember talking with her one time and she told me that she would often wonder if she would be accepted into medical school at her age, but then she admitted that at the time, it didn't matter. She said while she was pursuing her dream, she began to encounter experiences she could have never expected and she said that those are always the best, the experiences that are larger than what we can anticipate. Those are the experiences through which we truly grow. Her fulfillment was not the accomplishment of the degree, but through the development in earning it.

He seemed pleased hearing this and I was glad. For a while I had become a little distressed that I was being nothing but a free loader, that all I was doing was bumming rides from people and couldn't offer anything in return, but this instance gave me hope. I know it may not be the case with every ride, but at least this time I was able to give this man something in return even if what I gave him was only a story about someone else, a story of a part of my aunt's life, but a story that fit differently into each of our lives

He dropped me off at a place called Fish Lake which was the closest landmark to the Pacific Crest Trail that I could find on the road atlas. He insisted on taking a photograph of me and he asked if I wouldn't mind if he watched me walk away.

I can't say for certain how I may have looked to him as I disappeared into the forest and dissolved into the thickening green, but I do know what it looked like to me.

To him it may have looked like a picture perfect image, but I had the toughest time finding the trail. There were all types of logging roads and as I followed them, I kept turning in circles and I didn't have the faintest idea where I was and whether I was getting closer to the trail or farther away.

Then I realized the silliness in following the roads. They weren't built as much to travel in a specific direction and sustain that direction, they were cut through the woods with the intention of accessing specific plots for harvesting. On the other hand, the Pacific Crest Trail is continuous all the way from the border of Mexico to the border of Canada and I was certain that I was west of the trail. So I abandoned the roads and pulled out the plastic compass I bought at the supermarket in Reno and started walking east. I had to find it eventually and I did.

It was fairly late in the day so I only climbed a few miles up the trail above the pass. I noticed the patches of snow beginning to grow while I rose in elevation. Then the next day, those patches of snow kept growing larger and larger. Then there weren't any patches of snow, there were just patches of bare ground in the snow. Continuing to climb, those patches of bare ground began to shrink until they were gone and there was nothing but snow.

This surprised me. After all, it was almost May at the time and being from Alabama, I didn't expect there to be snow everywhere. At that point I figured I had walked at least eight miles and there was no sense turning back. I didn't realize I had to walk another eighty miles or more before I crossed another road. I ended up trudging for eight days over the mountains through the snow.

It was magnificent though. I didn't see a single footprint of another person, but I saw tracks of elk and other animals at times. There was one point which was the highest elevation of that section where the trail ascended a ridge and surmounted Devil's Peak before dipping back into the forests. As I climbed, having abandoned trying to follow the trail, I clambered over the rock outcroppings on the edge of the ridge. I could see the line of the ridge curve toward the peak like a horse shoe so I had some sense of where I was going, or thought I did. Fortunately I was approaching the peak from the south because if I would have tried to climb the north face of the ridge through the snow it would have been far more of a challenge.

While I was walking along the ridge I began to be concerned about causing an avalanche. I don't know the least bit about mountaineering. Really, I don't know the least bit about camping. All I had was a couple of loaves of bread, some peanut butter, jelly and several packages of dried noodles. I didn't even have a flash light. But then, at one point along the ridge, I saw some tracks. They must have been a coyote's, but they were huge, as big as a wolf's. The tracks traveled directly up the slope without making any cutbacks and then descended straight down the other side. I thought that this must be the method of doing it, after all, this was that animal's home and he or she would definitely know better than I, because that is how it survives. I thought that if I walked down the slope at an angle, I could trip a pressure point that was supporting a bank of snow and that would be the absolute worst place to be if that entire bank slid off the side of the mountain and directly on top of me. So when I reached the north face of the mountain where there was nothing but a pristine slope of snow, I barreled straight down.

This was fun, but afterwards there was a very insightful event or rather several events that opened my eyes to a reality of my life. Since the trail was buried beneath snow, it was extremely difficult to follow through the woods. There were markers on the trees but these weren't very frequent, so most what I had to go on was my compass and the lay of the land. As I would wander away from the path, I would often walk over trees that had fallen and were covered with snow. As the trees decomposed, they melted the snow around them and made small snow caves that I couldn't see. Then when I stepped on top of one, I would fall right through. It must have happening to me several dozen times a day. I would be merrily tramping along, and then all of the sudden, fwoomph, I was up to my neck in snow. Then I'd struggle to climb back out with the weight of the pack on my back.

Several times I became angry. I started blaming the trail. I started blaming everything. I didn't say anything out loud, even though I was alone, but I would rave in my head. Then at one point I stopped and after calming my thoughts, I did say something out loud. I stopped blaming the world and I said something to myself, as if I was speaking to someone else, as if I was speaking to a part of myself that I was ready to accept. I said, "Weldon, you are the one who made this choice. There is no one responsible for what you are doing but yourself. There is no one within a hundred miles of you. You are all alone. If you want to survive, you must save your own life."

I did make it through too, obviously, otherwise you wouldn't be receiving this letter until at least sometime after the winter's thaw and the forest filled with hikers and someone found this note in my lifeless, outstretched hand reaching for you.

One of the most spectacular events was after the last night before completing this section of the trail. I did my typical bundling in my sleeping bag and placed a sweat shirt over my head. That night it snowed again and I was completely buried. When I awoke in the morning, I realized that I was covered in snow, but this didn't bother me a bit. In fact, I felt a strange sense of peace and stillness. I calmly laid there for a minute and I did wonder if I would be able to get out, if the snow had buried me so that I might not be able to break through to the surface. The sweatshirt was still over my face and I couldn't see any light. But even thinking this, I wasn't concerned. I felt at ease. Then after a while, I suppose more through curiosity than concern for myself, I wiggled my arm up and poked through the snow above my face and the light was brilliant. I felt like I was cracking an egg from the inside and emerging into a bright new day.

Then I dug up my pack and rolled up my sleeping bag and made the last ascent and suddenly I found myself at the rim of Crater Lake. The sight was breathtaking. The crater is at the top of a volcano that erupted most recently about 8,000 years ago. The eruption was powerful enough to eject rocks out of the atmosphere. I couldn't help but wonder how many of those rocks have fallen into the sun by now and how many of them are still plunging through the immensity of space.

It is morning now and I am toward the base of the mountain. I am immersed in a wonderful world of lush life. There is a small creek tumbling down the mountain, splashing as softly as sweet laughter over the mossy stones.

Everywhere the ground juts into the air in plush, breathing green. I know this scrawl on the page is even less than the tracks of the coyote compared to the magnificence of the living being flowing like a ghost over the snow, but right now, it is the only way I can share this moment with you and I can't think of anything else I would rather do.

Your Friend,

Weldon

Dear Zoë,

Talking with you the other day was wonderful. I was walking through a town and had some change and I couldn't resist calling. Thank you for your offer about calling collect, but I couldn't do that. I could not allow myself to do anything at your expense. I must admit though, I wanted to hear if you had read my last letter. You probably have it now. I am not sure what would have caused the delay in you receiving it. It is nice to think, that perhaps while I am writing this, you might be reading that letter. I feel foolish too because I didn't even thank you for the letter you wrote me in Reno. I think I've read it a hundred times, and that was just this morning.

After my last hike, I've decided to take a short break. For some reason Dostoyevsky's name kept appearing in my head. Then when I was walking through a town, and as I passed by a bookstore, under the eaves outside they had a rack of old paperbacks and when I glanced over my eyes landed directly upon one of his books. I had to buy it and I've decided to camp for a little while and read it through.

I have found a nice place for the time being. It is off the road along side a creek and there is a perfect camping place beneath a huge Douglass Fir. The tree is a giant. There are some railroad tracks nearby and I have walked along them a couple of miles to a store where I can get food when I'm hungry.

The creek is nice company. It reminds me of the creek near my parents' house. I would spend hours every day along side that creek when I was younger. In some ways, that creek taught me a lot about narrative lines. I would learn every swirling eddy and the lay of the shoals and follow the arrangement of rocks and the flow of the current. Then after every storm, I would love to rush down to the banks to see how it changed. In time, the muddy water would clear as the storm's swell receded and slowly a new creek would appear. The shoals would have shifted, the rocks rearranged, the current changed. It constantly changed.

I loved finding the animals too. My favorites were always the turtles. I love them for their patience, their perseverance, their calm, curious stare. I love them for their composure. They have everything they need, even carrying their home on their backs. Then whenever they want to rest or sleep, they just draw back into their shells and are safe. What really seems magical though is after watching their cumbrous steps upon the ground, when they slip into the water, it is like they fly. Their burden is lifted from them and they elegantly dance, sometimes with the tips of their toes barely touching the silt that they stir from the river's bed as if adding a flourish to their flight.

My recent hike to Crater Lake seemed to change my attitude in many ways. What is most remarkable is how I eat. Before, I would gobble my meals as if I was rushing through some begrudged obligation. I didn't enjoy my meals. I would hardly notice them. I just ate to fill an emptiness and avoid the discomfort of hunger.

Now I eat slowly, chewing every bite until it is practically liquefied. I savor every subtle flavor to taste how the distinct ingredients blend into ever changing combinations and arrangements. Even the sight of a prepared meal appears sacred. In a way, it is like the practice of appreciation. Most of the times in my life, I had always taken the availability of food as a given and never thought how precious the sustenance is and all that is involved in providing it. It reminded me of a book I read by Joseph Campbell while I was in high school. He mentioned the importance of prayer before meals, how it was a conscious effort of a person to acknowledge what had been given. It is an expression of gratitude. After all, there is no doubt that many animals and plants have given their lives so that I may survive. Then this makes me wonder, what is given of my life, what does my life sustain and enable to survive?

Prayer has been a touchy subject for me for a while. I used to pray intensely when I was a child. I have had insomnia since I was very young and there was nothing else to do while laying in the dark for hours but think that there might be something else beyond what little I understood. It is instinctive to believe there is something treacherous in the darkness, that there are monsters lurking in the unknown, that there is danger beyond what we can see. But I thought there may be something good, something to be understood. So as a tiny child I spoke into the opening and wondered if there may be an answer.

Then when I was about fourteen, I noticed that all I did when I prayed was ask for things or insight or beg for forgiveness. It seemed arrogant. It seemed like a silly type of magic, as if I was trying to subjugate some supernatural powers to fulfill my will, satisfy my desires and resolve my mistakes. Now I feel that instead of asking for what I want, I will utilize what I have been given. I don't pray for salvation. I praise life by living and by fulfilling my potential. I feel my worthiness is proven in what I become while accepting that every accomplishment will present me with greater challenges.

The other night, I had an astonishing incident. I still don't have a flash light, so I bed down early and watch the stars overhead and think until my thoughts thicken into syrupy sleep. For some reason, or the lack there of, the other night I was fidgeting with my fingers on my chest. The sound of the fidgeting was making a crinkling and rummaging sound on top of the sleeping bag. An owl apparently mistook this for a mouse foraging on the ground and flew right over me. I didn't hear a sound because they have specially adapted feathers so they may fly silently and not startle their prey, but I felt the wind of its flight curl in eddies of air right over my nose and brush across my lips. For a moment, it was like a blink of the starry sky as its broad wings flew right over my face. Fortunately, it was able to figure out at the last moment that my fingers were in fact not a mouse, because I am sure having an owl's talons sunk in one's hands would be a smarting pain. I'm sure the owl would have been terrified too when it realized it grabbed something that would not easily be lifted from the earth. Still it was amazing, to come so close and practically touch an owl in flight with my nose while lying completely still.

My dreams at night have been interesting while I've been gone. Many of them involve conflict. I keep dreaming that I am fighting, although I do not know with whom or for what. There is a difference from my dreams before though. I am not stuck in the thick, viscous liquid that I usually move through in my dreams, stumbling in clumsiness through an inescapable resistance. Instead I move freely and effortlessly like a prize fighter. Other times, I dream of debating with people. I keep arguing particular points about William Blake's poetry and mythology, but I haven't the faintest idea with whom I'm debating or why.

Last night I had the most fascinating dream. I was standing in a long line at a soup kitchen. I have been to some places that are similar when I've briefly stayed at missions but I couldn't recognize this one. While I waited in line, I looked over to my left and I saw you. You were sitting in a chair staring at me and you had the saddest expression on your face. I can't believe what I did though. I saw you right next to me, only a few steps away and I stayed in the line and kept shuffling toward the ladled servings of soup. I can't imagine what more sustenance I could ever need but to comfort you.

Looking back, I think that it was a silly dream. That in reality, what I would have done, what I would like to do so much, was step out of that grungy line and walk directly to you. I would have dropped to my knees and lifted your tender hands with mine. Then I imagine lifting you from that sullen chair and off your feathery feet and jumping straight up into the sky with you in my arms, rising with cumulous clouds and gently laying you down in a place where the sun always shines and the air is warm and clear. And then brushing your hair from your face and tenderly kissing you while I lay down at your side, I would warmly press our bodies together so that nothing in the world could come between us and every inch of our being embraces and our lives overlap and flow like rivers as we run our course together and pour toward the immensity of the sea.

I will break off now. My fingers are numb from pressing on the pen. I like it though. There are little indentations that are left on my fingers tips for a while. It is like I have been pressing against something I wish to pass, something I wish to travel through and perhaps this obstacle is my distance from you.

Your Friend,

Weldon

Dear Zoë,

You would love my grandmother. I have been staying with her in Oregon City for a few weeks while I wait for the snow to melt in the mountains, then I will return to the wilderness. She is my mom's mom, or I suppose you could say my maternal grandmother, but I like the sound of "mom's mom." It sounds much warmer, like one soft layer snuggly covering another in secure, nurturing comfort. I had to pause in writing this letter for a moment to say it over and over and feel how the sound fills my mouth with a lulling hum. If anyone walked by they would probably think I am crazy as I repeat these sounds to myself. Or maybe they would think a humming bee is trapped in the flower of my mouth. Sometimes I become consumed with the sensation of shaping the sounds of words. Their audible forms are much different than the stick figures of this script.

Anyway, my grandmother is a wonderful lady. We sit for hours as she tells me stories. She is fiercely independent too, almost to a fault. The other day, I went to the grocery store for her so she wouldn't have to carry the bags back and when I returned, she was cutting the lawn in front of her trailer. I scolded her, although in the teasing way we often talk, because I think she sent me to the store on purpose so she could cut the lawn and not have to ask me, or rather elude my insistence of doing it for her. I had to tell her that I was her grandson and I should be the one doing that for her. She had already done her job raising my mom and my uncles. It was her turn to relax. It was her turn to be taken care of.

While I'm staying, my uncle has been nice enough to let me work at his place to earn a little money. He owns a strawberry field outside of town. He said it would be good to utilize my expertise in landscaping since I had done that work before, and I am planting rose bushes around his house and fruit trees for a small orchard.

Looking over the strawberry fields fills me with a strange sensation though. They have just planted this year's crop and I can see the tiny, tender shoots emerging from the rich soil. I have fun looking back at the rows and observing how the furrows' repetition changes as I move around in the yard. I know each row is practically the same, but from each place I stand, they all look different. A few rows will line up with my sight and extend straight along the length of the field, but the others will angle in strange rhythms like the shimmering and pulsating texture of the silk weave of fabric. Unlike a silk fabric though, in this case the threads are little sprouts of life so this field will arise like a butterfly into thousands upon thousands of little juicy rubies of fruit. I know the furrows all line up in neat rows and if I saw the field from the sky, I would see this directly, but from where I stand on the ground, I can only see a couple of the rows at a time as I move to plant one pear tree after another.

It is strange at times because I can almost see my mom out in the fields working. She told me several times, and believe me she would not let me forget, that she had spent most of her summers as a child out in the strawberry fields picking with her brothers and parents. I forget exactly how much she said she'd make, but I think it was something like a couple of dimes a day. At the time they had little choice; they were struggling to survive. She would give the dimes she had earned to her parents after the sun had set and day began to darken and cool.

Zoë

It is painful for me to imagine her doing this. The strawberry bushes are really short so it is easiest to crawl while you're working and I can see my mom as a tender five year old child crawling through the dirt and dragging the crates behind her. The worst thing, although I know my grandparents would have never done it, is how many of the children would be slapped around by their parents when the strawberries they brought to the weighing station were bruised.

When I was thinking about this though, I remembered something that I wrote to you in a letter before. It was the story of when I was a kid and I told my mom that I never wanted to have children. Now I think how her hearing that must have bruised her. For a mother to hear her child make such a statement and see the pain that small child feels, she might easily begin to blame herself, she might begin to believe somehow she had inadvertently caused that pain.

Now this puzzling statement seems to be more of a source of shame. For years I had thought that I was making this statement from an uncorrupted state of mind as a young child. That in a small way, I was resolved to alleviate the suffering in the world. Now, I realize that I made the statement out of a pure lack for consideration. I was only thinking of myself, of my own childish desire to end the discomfort I felt. I was only considering what I felt, without considering my need to feel, not just to feel what I wanted, but to feel reality. Now in accepting this statement and my shame in saying it, instead of cowering behind the shame, I open my life with it. I accept it with some degree of understanding and now wonder what else I am overlooking and ignoring.

I try to remind myself that I am always overlooking something. In fact, from what little I recognize, I accept that I am always overlooking nearly everything. I remember once when I was a child, I was walking through the woods and passed a bush. Inside the bush, right next to me was a tiny bird. I was almost startled when I saw it and I couldn't believe it had not flown away. It was so close I could reach and touch it and although it was delicately perched on a twig, it was still as a stone. It didn't seem real because in every experience I had had before with birds, they had always flown away when I approached. I then realized that it had thought itself completely hidden and figured I would walk past without noticing. Then I considered how often I had actually passed birds in the bush and never noticed. I realized how much I must be missing, convinced of my vision, but really only recognizing what I am expecting.

Working in the hot sun today, remembering these distant memories, I pictured in my mind the sadness and hurt that must have fallen over my mother's face when she heard me make that statement as a child. At the time, I couldn't see this. I had not opened my eyes wide enough to begin recognizing anyone else. I only felt myself.

Then while I was considering this, I looked out in the field and it was like I could see my mother as a child wiping the sweat from her brow with the back of her tiny hand and she looked up at me and I saw her smile preciously.

Your Friend,

Weldon

July 12

Dear Zoë,

The picture you sent is beautiful, or rather, you are more beautiful in the picture than I remember. Wait that still isn't right. See, it is still difficult for me to say what I mean. Can't I just say that you are beautiful without trying to compare you with something else? Can't I just see your beauty for what it is in itself? Thank you for sending the photo.

I hope you don't mind, but I have been keeping it in the book that I am reading. I was wondering if you might be offended by this and I tried to think it through and I thought perhaps it is like a flower preserved between the pages, but I know this isn't right, because I wouldn't want to try binding you in a book; I only want you to live your life as you would choose. Plus, if I thought your picture was a flower, it would have to be plucked and that would even be worse. In a way though, I thought it might be showing you what I'm reading at the time, and in that way, showing you a portion of me.

Your letters are wonderful. Thank you for writing and

73

sending them. I read them constantly. I can almost hear you speaking. I close my eyes and repeat the lines that I have practically memorized and I try to imagine you here with me. Thank you for sharing your thoughts.

I have left Oregon City now and have been hiking through the wilderness again. The sights are magnificent. I bought a little gas camping stove at a hardware store which allows me to cook oatmeal and macaroni and cheese. Although it is summer now, it gets cold clambering over the ridges in the mountains and the warm meals are comforting.

The cascades are an amazing string of volcanoes. Day after day while I hike, I will see one looming ahead of me, slowly growing larger with each glimpse I gain through the thick forests and then suddenly I find myself standing at its base while it rises above me tremendously. Then I walk around it and it slowly recedes behind me while another rises up ahead.

I am sorry that I haven't written more lately. You would think that I have all the time in the world to scribble a note and I hope you haven't worried, but I still have not bought a flashlight. In fact I don't even have a tent which might be absurd since I'm hiking in what is practically a temperate rainforest. But someone who gave me a ride gave me a tarp because he thought I was bonkers hiking without any cover. And then I bought a $2 string hammock. When it doesn't rain, I just sleep on the ground. When it does rain though, I string up the hammock and the tarp over my head and I stay high and dry undercover. Plus, it is probably lighter than a tent, not to mention cheaper. With the money I have, the less I spend, the longer I can go without needing to stop and get a job. So I stretch every cent as far as I can.

The best time for me to write would be at night but without a flashlight this is impossible, unless you wanted to try reading letters with scrawled lines blindly wandering illegibly over the pages. In that case, instead of describing my wanders, the sprawling script would be more of an illustration and even more difficult, if not impossible, to follow.

I walk through the daylight hours. Then I lay out my sleeping bag, cook a quick meal of macaroni and cheese and settle to sleep. I never bother building a fire. It seems a waste. I am plenty warm bundled in my bag and although a fire can provide a bright light, one can only see a few feet, where as in the dark, I can see all the way to the stars.

Right now, I am off the trail. At the major mountain passes, I will typically stop and hitchhike into the nearest town, buy provisions and unload my trash in a dumpster. This time, when I headed into a town, someone told me about a fair that was going on outside of Eugene and I thought I would check it out.

The fair was interesting. It is a counter culture festival that has been held every summer since the early 70's. I got a job with one of the crews that clears the recycling bins and doing this, they fed me and I got to visit the fair for free.

There were many booths that were fascinating with people discussing all types of alternative energy and various ideas concerning social formulation and theory, but I must say, for the most part, I am disappointed. There are so many people at the fair who seem to romanticize the past, the old hunter/gathering lifestyles with the inevitably strict tribal social hierarchies that are a bit absurd. To me, society has progressed beyond this.

No doubt, I am getting a first hand account of the

struggles of living in the wild. I have to admit, that being able to turn a faucet handle and instantly have a rush of warm water is a luxury I have learned to appreciate. Most of the time, I get fairly grungy and I am definitely not in the state that I would like for you to see me. I do bath in the wild, jumping into the cold rivers spilling from the snow melt in the mountains, but sometimes I feel sorry for the people that give me rides in their cars because I know I must reek.

I wouldn't say this is entirely bad though, or at least for the time being. I remember when I first arrived at my grandmother's house, she had me take a shower immediately. While I was washing, I could see how the water became gritty with the dirt as it rinsed off of me. The sight of this made me feel like I was really refreshing myself, that I was being renewed. But then, every day after this while I stayed with her, even after days of hard work at my uncles, I would get into the shower and the water washing from my body would remain clear. I felt I was accomplishing nothing by bathing. The water was only clouded with the suds of soap. It seemed like I couldn't feel clean unless I allowed myself to be dirty first.

This probably sounds a little disgusting and now I feel a little embarrassed to send you the letter. If you see me again, I promise you that I will be bathed and I will be wearing clean clothes. This does make me want to confess something to you. I want to tell you that I am still a virgin. I don't know what you think of this. I know for guys, it is often frowned upon and a source of shame. I don't know if you are and this doesn't matter to me. Ray never said anything about you two like that; he was always a gentleman and never stooped to any type of boastful buffoonery. I guess that was one of the reasons that I admired him. He was strong enough that he didn't need the typical affirmation that others always sought.

You don't have to respond to this the next time we talk. In fact, I feel I shouldn't have mentioned it. Like I said, it doesn't really matter to me, but I wanted to be forthright with you. I want to show you what I really am and this is something that I know for sure.

Your Friend,

Weldon

Zoë

Post Script

I usually read over my letters before I seal them in an envelope. That explains why there are always so many scratched out words and corrections. I hope my letters don't give you a terrible impression that I am a jumbled and scrambled person, although I often feel I am. But I am a little nervous about rereading this letter. I am wondering if I may have overextended myself and I hope I might not give you a bad impression of me. I have decided that I will finish this brief explanation and seal the letter in an envelope, then address it and place a stamp on it, so one way or another you will receive it. But I will give myself some more time to consider whether I will mail it to you. Perhaps I might decide to give it to you in person and then you can read it while I am with you, or I could read it to you.

Dear Zoë,

Please forgive me for taking so long to write. I am still in the wilderness and have been for months. Right now I am at the Columbia Gorge and just walked over the bridge of the gods. The name is from a Native American legend. There are three volcanoes in the immediate area. Mount Adams is the biggest of the three and stands north of the gorge somewhat close to Mount St. Helens. Mount Hood stands south of the gorge. The Native Americans believed the mountains were gods. From my experiences standing at their bases and even climbing toward their peaks, I wouldn't argue against this. In this myth Mount Adams is married to Mount St. Helens, but Mount Hood continues to court her. He can't cross the Columbia River though, so he made a landslide that completely dammed the river to allow him to cross each night to visit her.

The landslide really occurred thousands of years ago and completely dammed the river and consequently created a great lake. Then eventually the water filled to crest the edge of the landslide. At first there was only the slightest trickle, but this deepened and opened into a rush that became torrential as the dam washed away. What remained were the more dense rocks that made a cataract of rapids. Now the river has been dammed by the Bonneville Dam and the rapids submerged, but the highway engineers built a cantilever bridge that spans the water and I walked across this. To make the bridge lighter, the engineers made the road from metal grating, so while I walked across I could see straight down to the river below. What was odd though, they still made me pay the bridge toll and there was no pedestrian walkway, so I couldn't have been paying for the accommodations made for my mode of transportation. I had to dodge the cars while I walked across, but I guess it was still worth it because it was easier than swimming.

In one of the sections of the Pacific Crest Trail, I bumped into a gentleman who was from California and with whom I hiked a few days. He is a fascinating man. He said that he often takes the summers off when he begins putting on too many pounds and hikes the trail. He said he has walked the entire trail several times, but in increments over the years and often returns to some of his favorite sections.

In this way, I suppose you could think of it as a book that you might have and after reading the long narrative line meandering through various episodes and imbroglios while weaving together the lives of the characters, you can return back to various sections and read through your favorite parts.

He is an avid reader and at one point I was telling him about some of the books I'd read and some of the books that I thought I should reread. He said that I was too young to worry about rereading books. I don't completely agree with this, but then he said something that really astonished me. He said that he always found it interesting to reread books that he had read when he was younger, because although the books haven't changed, the reading always does. And in this way, the books show him how he has changed and from a different angle how much he is the same, then he said - and most importantly how much more he is the same.

One night after we ate, we were talking about various poets and of course I started ranting about William Blake like I was set upon making one of my twisted dreams come true. At one point, he recited a poem to me. It is called

"And Death Shall Have No Dominion" by Dylan Thomas. I asked him to recite it so many times that he started getting a little annoyed, which surprised me because I would have never expected my persistence could annoy such a patient and kind person, but I suppose I can be more persistent than I realize.

Eventually though, we split up. I reached Mt. Hood. At the mountain, the trail rises above the tree line and while I walked, a storm began blowing in. Since I was above the trees, I couldn't string my tarp up anywhere, so I decided to climb above the storm. By the time the storm arrived, I was above it. I stood in the crisp, cool air without knowing the turbulence that whirled below. I could see the peaks of other mountains and they looked like tiny islands in an ocean of condensation.

That night I slept up toward the top of the mountain, although I wasn't able to make it to the very peak. At one point I was shimmying along a cliff and had to get past a boulder and while I was trying to pass it, it became dislodged which was a bit frightening. Believe me, you do not want to be stuck a hundred feet up on a cliff straddling a boulder that you are precariously balancing. Of course I couldn't stand there balancing it forever, so I lunged to the side and jumped further down the ledge and this huge rock swiveled with a gravelly grind and then tumbled silently into the open air before splashing into a bank of snow below.

At that point I officially suspended my campaign for the mountain's summit. I sat for hours on the ledge looking over the north face of the mountain that was covered with glaciers furrowed with deep mysterious crevices that slipped with the most majestic blue before plummeting into the deep darkness. While I sat I could hear rocks on the mountain falling. I couldn't see them, but I could hear them tumbling and knocking as they skipped along the steeps in their precipitous falls. I knew it was simply erosion or that's what we call it, but to me, it didn't sound like the mountain was crumbling; it sounded like it was growing, like I could feel the pulsing of the veins of molten rock swelling within, pushing the mountain higher and the rocks that were falling were like bark on a tree flaking away to accommodate the new growth.

Zoë

While I sat on this ledge, the title of that poem kept echoing in my head, "And Death Shall Have No Dominion." Even though I had the gentleman repeat the poem more times than I can count, I didn't even try to recall any of the specific lines. The entire poem fit together marvelously and developed like life itself, growing rhythmically, persistently, indomitably, and beautifully, each line depicting the scattered pieces of particular faults and failures then melding them all into images and ideas of glorious endurance and triumph. I thought that if I tried to recall any single piece, the whole I felt within might collapse. I hope you look the poem up. You probably have some of his poetry already. I wouldn't be surprised. I can almost see the book in your shelf. But if you do read it, please read it out loud. I know we're far away from one another, but I will try to listen carefully. I would love to hear you singing those lines and I think I can, if I can only stay at the top of this mountain.

Your Friend,

Weldon

Dear Zoë,

Our last conversation on the phone meant more to me than you could ever know. I didn't want to say anything while we talked, but the truth is, I was calling you from jail. At the time I was talking with you I was cradling the phone in my hands that were cuffed together. I was seated at a desk with police officers.

First and foremost, I want to explain something about what I said. When you told me that you wanted to drive out to meet me and be with me, there was no way I could say yes. As much as I wanted to be with you, as much as I still want to be with you, I could never do this to you. I know from the letters I might make what I'm doing sound very sensational and liberating, and in ways it is, but it is more than that and I would never want to make you throw your life away like I feel I may be doing with my own.

While I was in jail, I read quite a number of books. In fact, that is practically all I did. I would lay in bed reading and I would fall asleep reading. Then while I slept, I would make the stories up in my head while I dreamed. I was

87

hardly reading though. Mostly, my eyes were glossing over the pages while I mulled and roiled in my thoughts as I tried to recollect what happened.

I was stupid, stupid, stupid, stupid! I got drunk. For some reason I thought it would be a good idea to stop at a bar and have some drinks. I had spent months walking across the entire state of Oregon and half of Washington, then I hitchhiked back to Nevada to withdraw some of the money I still had in the bank from working in Reno and I thought I would celebrate. I hitchhiked to another state and stopped in a town and found a bar. Of course, I went about it heavy handed, buying people drinks, shooting whiskey and then I blacked out. The next thing I knew, I woke up in jail and had no idea what I had done until after the arraignment.

What happened that night is still uncertain to me. I was in jail for two weeks. At one point they took me to a psychiatric hospital for an evaluation. They gave me an examination then they returned to the room with the diagnosis and with a sneer they said that I lived in a fantasy world. I looked at them and said, "You all should look around. Every single thing that we are surrounded with in this room, in fact the room itself, is a substantiated idea. All these objects are a fabrication of someone's imagination. We all live in a fantasy world." Of course they did not like this and sent me directly back to jail.

Eventually I went to court and I stood before the judge and apparently a lot of things happened that night. They told me that if I was willing to sign a release of culpability form, they would release me with only the minimum fines for the charges. So I paid $60 and they told me to get out of the state and released me. They even gave me a ride to the bus station.

While I was in jail, though, something startling occurred to me. For the last year I have been wandering about the country feeling completely liberated. All those binding strings that have been tying my life down have been cut. From all those dreams of fighting, whatever it was I was fighting in my mind has been beaten countless times. But then, all of the sudden, all that freedom I felt was taken away. I went from soaring like a bird through the sky to locked in a cage with 15 other guys, crammed together in bunk beads in a 14 X 14 room behind bars. Apparently I was on the third floor, but for all I knew, I was ten thousand feet underground. It was not nice. It was not one of the newer jails with cinder blocks and solid steel doors and a room to yourself. It was a mob of us crammed together inside a cage. And there were lines of cages stacked one on top of the other in the steel clacking dark.

When I called, there is no way I could have told you what had happened to me, even if I knew, and there was no way I would tell you where I was. I did not want to subject you to what I was experiencing. I didn't want you to know where I was. I did not even want your thoughts to be with me in there. I just thought that if there is one last voice that I want to hear in my life, I wanted that voice to be yours.

You will see from the postage stamp that I am mailing this from somewhere outside of the Great Basin National Park. I bought a bus ticket here and I am walking back into the wilderness. I feel safe there. I feel ashamed to write this letter to you. I need time to think and be alone. Please don't worry about me. Don't wait for me. I don't want to keep you holding onto some hope that I may never live up to. It is shameful to think that I have done this to you while I've wandered aimlessly around the past year. Find someone who can really care for you. Find someone who can be there for you. Find someone who can love you. That is what you deserve more than anything else. You don't deserve someone like me. I'm sorry.

W. Keyes

Dearest Zoë,

I do not know how the last letter made you feel. I know that I was hurting very badly when I wrote it and if I displaced my misery upon you, that would be a shame, my shame. I can only hope that you are not so upset that you threw this letter away without opening it. I know this may be the case and if it is, I can understand perfectly well. In fact, it is really easy for me to envision this envelop fluttering into a trash can and lying unopened on the top of the heap before piles of rubbish and refuse are dumped on top of it. I can see myself buried silently within it. I can see that I deserve this.

If you are reading this though, which I can only hope you are, I want to tell you what happened to me while I was in the Great Basin Park. However saying this now, I feel a bit sickened; I feel like I'm pleading in front of you demanding, "Me, Me, Me. Listen to me, listen to me." I feel obnoxious. I feel disgusting. However if you are able to bear with me one last time, it will be the last I will ask of you.

The bus dropped me off at the entrance of the park and a park ranger was kind enough to give me a ride inside. She was returning to the park from her weekend off. She asked me what I was doing and I told her that I was planning to hike around for a few days. Somehow, I mentioned that I didn't have a flashlight. She said it was crazy to go camping in the wilderness without one. She insisted I take one she had in her car and eventually I accepted.

The first couple of days were spent ascending a ridge. I reached an elevation higher than I had ever climbed before, over 13,000 feet, which is far from the top of Everest, but still, the air was thin and the sights were expansive. I followed the ridge for a while in a descent and above the normal tree line, I found something amazing. There is a tree called the Bristlecone Pine. When these trees grow below the tree line, they resemble most other conifers. But sometimes they grow above the tree line in extremely dry and rocky soil. When they grow in this particularly harsh environment, exposed to the wide open and buffeted by winds, they grow practically forever. They look like bonsai trees, except they are as big as houses. I touched some of the bigger ones that were older than the pyramids, older than Stonehenge, and they were still alive. They live for thousands of years. I have always admired the patience of the trees, but these single trees are older than human civilization.

I camped in the grove that night and I had the most magnificent dream. I didn't dream about arguing. I didn't dream about fighting. I had really become concerned about those dreams. I didn't know what I was fighting about. I didn't know what I was fighting for. I just felt like I was in some perpetual altercation. It made me think of that one scene in *The Battleship Potemkin* where everyone is rioting and brawling and everyone is so entangled and embroiled in the melee, they don't even notice the baby carriage rolling down the steps, perilously plunging down the stairs. The whole time you're thinking, what more could anyone be fighting for but life and everyone is so lost in the fight that they are all losing the life they believe they are trying to preserve.

But this night I dreamed something beautiful, something more beautiful than I could ever imagine. I was dreaming, but it was like I was lying on the ground underneath the stars as I had done so many nights of the past year. Then the stars began to move. They began whirling and swirling and then converged together into the shape of a person. And then I could see this shape was the figure of a lady. Then she began to descend and when she did, all of the sudden, the ground began to rise, the ground began to rise in mountains to meet her. And then as they did, they chiseled into palaces to receive her. She descended directly over me and held out her hand. She lifted me to my feet and we began walking. We ascended stairs cut from solid rock. My heavy steps clunked on the stone and she drifted over the steps effortlessly, floating above them, leading me by the hand.

Then we arrived at two massive doors that must have been twenty feet tall. It felt like I had seen those doors so many times, but had never seen what was on the other side. They were bolted and chained and locked and there seemed to be no way to pass. Then she calmly waved her hand and in her whisper I heard your voice and the doors were blown wide open. You were the lady. I didn't even realize how dark it had been where we stood until the doors opened and I had to cover my eyes from the bright light inside. Then I could see the most beautiful garden. It was a forest filled with magnificent trees and bursting with ferns and every luscious plant swaying with succulent fruits from the sweetest dreams. There was a menagerie of animals grazing through the meadow ahead and as the doors had burst open, they all perked in attention, their ears sharpened and their eyes opened wide. Then I noticed what they were seeing, I saw the reflection of you in all of their eyes and all their wariness from the startling commotion calmed and they tranquilly settled back into themselves.

Then you led me through the meadow and into the forest. I didn't notice at first, but as you held my hand in yours we began to float above the trees and rose high above them. The trees became so distant, they began to look like a single leaf, a tapestry of deepening green. Then as we drifted higher, we began to scatter into the stars in the sky and I discovered I was awake and staring into the starry night.

The next day I continued walking along the sharp ridge

then dipped into a ravine. I discovered a cave. I peeked inside, and then I remembered that the park ranger had given me a flashlight so I climbed in and began descending through its deepening passages. It was awkward carrying the backpack, so I grabbed a few things and set the pack down near the entrance. I had your photograph in the book that I was reading, so I grabbed it and put the book in my pocket and began exploring. I loved spelunking when I was young. I loved diving deep into caves and exploring the hushed hollows.

I walked as far as I could, flashing the light around the expansive chambers and following the smooth convolutions of the cave. Then I found another passage and followed it deeper. I felt like I was inside one of the Bristlecone Pines, walking through the centuries they have grown, following the thousands of years tiny drips of water have slowly carved this space from solid rock. At times I felt I was in one of the branches of the trees, the passage slowly narrowing, like I was crawling toward one of the tips of a twig where I might burst as a blossom into the sky. Other times, I felt I was descending along the roots nudging myself deeper through the thickening and tightening soil.

Finally I reach a point where I could crawl no longer. The passage narrowed tighter than I could squeeze. I flashed the light deeper, and it appeared as if the cave had ended, but it may have simply made a turn and descended more. I extended my arm through the hole trying to touch the further wall, trying to reach a completion. My whole body was pressed against the cold stone, the length of my arm plunging to touch something final, something conclusive, but my fingers only wiggled in space. I could press my palms upon the sides, but I could not touch an end.

Since I could go no further, I pulled the book from my pocket and gazed at your picture. I do not know how long I stared at it, but I became mesmerized. I may have been delirious, but at times it was like your hair was flowing in the pictures, sheens of light shimmering down the dark flow.

After a while I began reading more of the book. I had found the book on the Pacific Crest Trail. Someone had left it in a zip lock bag. The book is called *Arrowsmith* by Sinclair Lewis. In the book there is one line that profoundly engaged me. The character Martin Arrowsmith left college for a while during the great depression and hoboed around the country on trains. Finally at one point, he told himself, "I will not be a slave to freedom."

This line has been on my mind a lot. Like I said before, I have reached a point where I have cut every tie from my life. I have stripped myself to bare bone. I have detached myself from everything. At this point I was deep beneath the surface of the earth near the bottom of a cave and I was out of touch with everything. I was free from it all. There was practically nothing except the hard rock that completely surrounded me. And then I realized I have achieved the freest that I can ever be without dying. I am so free, I can do practically nothing; I am simply flailing in the emptiness that remains after I removed every contact and relation from my life. Without a single attachment I am in limbo.

Then at some point while I was reading I fell asleep. While I slept, I had another interesting dream. It involved William Blake, but this time I was not arguing about him, I was sitting right next to him. I could see him as clear as day. He had the kindest, calmest most soothing expression on his face like I had always imagined him and even when he had spoken of how he had died so many times, he still seemed to have this sparkling state of serenity in his eyes. He looked over at me and asked, "My friend, shall we commit ourselves to this void?"

At that point the dream disappeared from my mind as if covered with the stroke of a raven's wing. I was roused from my sleep, but it was like I could not open my eyes. I was completely blind. I didn't panic, but I was startled. Then I felt the cold stone. I felt my hands press against the rock beneath me and I could feel the slight grit against my palms. Then I remembered that I was in a cave. I felt around the ground and I found the flash light, but I had fallen asleep with it on and the batteries had expired. I was down deep in an unknown cave and had absolutely no light. There was no sound except my breathing and my hands clambering, groping in the darkness.

I had to do all I could to keep myself from panicking. I must admit, at the time that is all I felt I could do, remaining calm took every faculty of thought I possessed. I had to keep my senses about me, even if my primary sense, that is my sight, was completely worthless.

I began crawling out of the passage I had descended, trying to follow a vague memory, carefully feeling my way along the walls. This was very slow going, but it wasn't too difficult because of the narrowness of the passage. Then the passage began to widen so I would feel with one hand on the floor and keep another at the wall.

As I continued to crawl, I would try feeling the other side of the passage but it kept extending further away until I realized I was crawling back and forth across a wide chamber. I realized I had lost all sense of direction not even knowing the direction of the passage from which I had crawled, let alone the direction toward the exit. At this point I just laid there looking at nothing, hearing only silence and feeling only myself.

I rolled over on the floor and felt the book in my pocket and I remembered your picture. I pulled it out, but I couldn't see it. I could feel the glossy face of the paper, and I gently ran my fingertips over this hoping that some how, some way, I might distinguish some feature of your image. It felt like the cave was closing around me, as if the darkness was turning to stone. I began to consider the fact that I might die.

I fell asleep in exhaustion. I didn't recall any dreams, but when I woke I could hear water. There was a slow dripping. I began to distinguish little drops pattering over the stone. I tried to determine where they were coming from, but they seemed to be coming from everywhere. Although I knew that I was in terrible danger, it must have been raining outside and the cave could flood, I couldn't help noticing how beautiful the drops sounded. At first, they were simply pats on the rock, tiny splatters, and then little pools began to form and the droplets made musical sounds rippling through the darkness and resounding with the curvature of the cave's surface. I crawled to one of the tiny pools and drank of the water. I could even smell it. It smelled like the sky. It smelled like outside. Then for a second I thought I heard the sound of a river faintly in the distance. Then it stopped. In a few minutes, I heard it again and I realized, it wasn't a river, it was thunder.

Slowly I began to crawl toward the sound. I would stop and pause sometimes when I became uncertain, but then I would hear it again and it would sound louder. I knew then that I had finally found a way to lead me out.

I continued this way and then at one point while I was looking up for the sound, I saw the frame of the mouth of the cave flash with light. It was the flickering of lightening in the sky. I didn't see the bolt, but the light was so bright, it practically seared itself in my sight. For a minute, in every direction I looked, I could see the glowing mouth of the cave slowly fading. I kept crawling closer and the lightening lit up the entrance again. It was the most wonderful feeling stepping out into the rain. It felt like the entire world had opened up before me. It was still night, but then lightening would flash and for a flickering instant it would be bright as day. To get out of the rain, I crawled back into the mouth of the cave. I pulled out your picture and held it in my hand. With every flash of lightening, your face would suddenly brighten right before me. I swear every time lightening flashed, your smile lifted higher and felt kinder.

It feels strange writing this while I am now sitting outside in the warm sunshine. The storm has passed and I can look over my shoulder and see the mouth of the cave from where I emerged last night. I have decided that I am returning. After my last letter, I wouldn't be surprised if you never wanted to see me again. But I have realized something. A phrase came to mind while I was crawling through the cave, practically deprived of every sense I had of the world around me, knowing nothing but a dwindling thought of myself in a cold darkness, I kept saying, "I am ready to stop looking and start seeing."

Before I heard those rain drops seeping into the cave, I wasn't very far from the exit. Those hours I had spent crawling through the darkness had carried me close to where I needed to be. But without knowing where the exit was, even though I was close, I could have been a million miles away and it would have made no difference.

When I did find the exit of the cave, I knew it like nothing else, I could feel it, I could feel the relief and with that relief all I could think of was you. Now I know. I know I cannot be yours. I certainly don't want you to be mine. I could never own you. I would never want to. But I am hoping that maybe, just maybe, we may be together.

Zoë

Now more than ever before, I send this to you Zoë with my love,
Weldon

About the Author

Garrett Buhl Robinson was born and raised in Trussville, Alabama. At 14, he was enrolled at Fork Union Military Academy. Upon graduating, he briefly attended The University of the South in Sewanee, Tennessee. After leaving the university, he lived on the West Coast of the United States for twenty years, writing and studying independently while supporting himself at various jobs. He currently lives in New York City.

Other books by the author:

Nunatak, a novel

Martha (a poem)

www.garrettrobinson.us

New York City 4/11/15

ZOË

Garrett Buhl Robinson

For wondrous
+ Precious life.

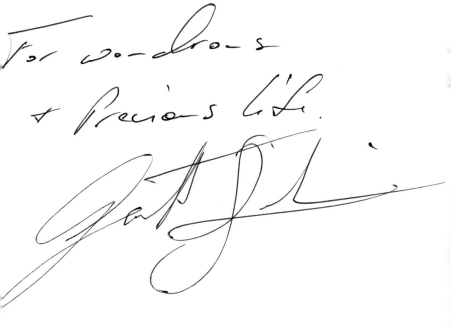

Made in the USA
Middletown, DE
27 December 2014